Beholding Baby Glisten, The Fairhope Dragon

Story by Debby Hackbarth

Illustrations by Carter Hlavin, Debby Hackbarth, and Jonah Hackbarth

Dedication:

To my husband, Jim, for his love, daily encouragement, and advice.

To my grandchildren, Katarina, Jonah, Carter, and Kaleb for their strength of character.

To John, for helping me to keep the dream alive.

Thanks:

To Carter and Jonah for their extremely talented artwork.

To Bekah, Katarina, and Jim for their editing assistance.

To the lovely city of Summerdale for permission to use their emblem.

Beholding Baby Glisten,

The Fairhope Dragon

The Fairhope dragon was ready to be born. Her parents, Aquamarine and Sunshine spent many hours building a comfortable nest for their baby's egg. Even among dragon eggs, it was fantastic to behold. It shone in iridescent yellow, lime green, and several shades of blue.

The brilliant hues of the egg
echoed the vivid coloring of the
parents' scales. Aquamarine, the
father, and Sunshine, the mother,
decided to call their baby Glisten
because her egg glistened or
sparkled in the sunlight.

Dragon eggs can take from one to two years to hatch. Due to the hot summer, Glisten started hatching after a year. Most hatchlings, or wyrmlings, are about the size of a medium-sized dog. However, Glisten was tiny, about the size of a small cat.

Glisten's parents were omnivores which means they ate animal protein and plants. Because they wanted Glisten to keep growing as rapidly as possible, they constantly brought her food: shrimp, birds, turtles and their eggs, and fresh grass.

Glisten's favorite food was popcorn, or grass, shrimp which grew in abundance in the Fish River and nearby Week's Bay. Her parents saw the joy on her face when she ate shrimp.

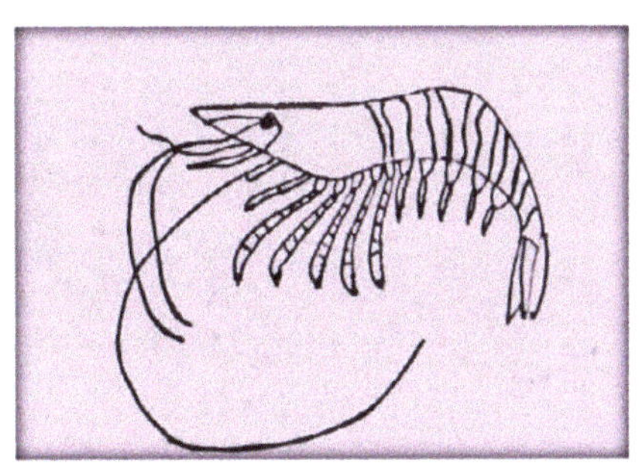

The dragon family slept inside an old barn located on the Fish River north of Week's Bay because they wanted to protect tiny Glisten. This barn belonged to Mariposa, a retired teacher, who taught science at Fairhope High School for many years.

Aquamarine, or Aqua, and Sunshine, or Sunny, enjoyed taking care of Glisten. They beheld or watched over her while she grew. Glisten loved to fly, play with her parents, and forage for food.

The dragons became increasingly afraid because they saw and heard humans when they flew and hunted for food. Fortunately, Mariposa used a small barn on her property and rarely visited the old barn where the dragons lived.

Aqua and Sunny decided to move Glisten north toward Clay City and Summerdale before Mariposa could discover them. They pushed straw over the area where the egg hatched before they left. Glisten always remembered the farm where she was born.

A few years after the dragons left
the Fish River area, a young
couple from Fairhope moved into
a small farm close to Mariposa.
The couple, Susy and Gary, met at
Fairhope High School. Susy was
raised in Fairhope, and Gary's
family farmed on twenty acres
east of Fairhope.

The couple married the summer after their high school graduation. The following summer, Susy had twins: Kaleb and Katarina. Both sets of grandparents were overjoyed to take care of the beautiful twins when Susy and Gary started college to study for their veterinary technician certifications.

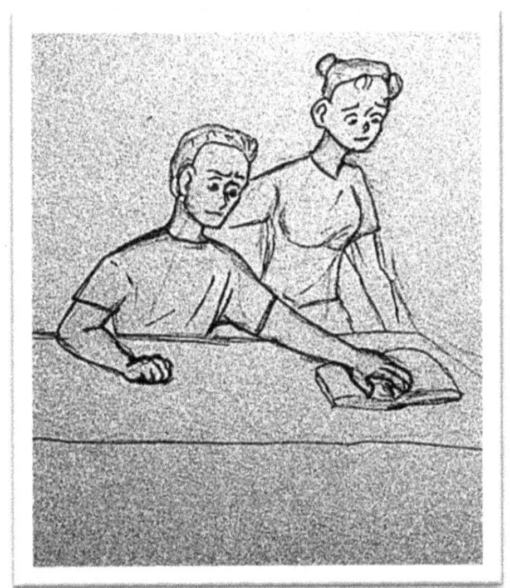

After graduation, the young couple worked at the Baldwin Humane Society. Susy and Gary loved working at the Humane Society; however, they wanted to spend more time with the twins in rural Fairhope.

The twins' grandparents got together and mortgaged a small farm on the Fish River. Now, the young family could live in the country to build their young family, grow crops, and raise animals.

Even at a young age, the twins wanted to be outside all the time. Susy taught the children how to feed the goats and chickens. Gary brought them to the family's roadside stand where the twins helped stack vegetables into baskets.

Katarina and Kaleb thrived in the warm Alabama climate where they could grow organic food year-round and fish in the nearby river. They grew close, as twins often do, and loved to spend time with their grandparents.

A few years later, Susy's parents moved north to take care of other family members. A few months after Susy's parents moved, Gary's parents were killed in a boating accident. These events brought Kaleb, Katarina, Gary, and Susy even closer together.

As the twins neared their sixth birthday, Gary gave them more responsibility at the roadside stand. Kaleb and Katarina designed signs, carried and stacked produce, and watched as Gary sold goods and made change for customers.

Susy, Gary, and the twins were content with farm life. At the twins sixth birthday party, Susy's parents came for a visit. The grandparents told Susy they could no longer pay the mortgage. Consequently, Gary and Susy decided to sell the farm.

Gary and his family bought a home on an acre, next to Mariposa. As the family settled into a new routine, they loved to pick berries every morning, when in season.

One morning, when the twins
were seven, the family left to go
pick berries. Gary and Susy taught
the twins to watch for snakes in
the bushes. This morning, however,
the adults did not see snakes in
the bushes. A venomous snake bit
Gary and then Susy.

The parents shouted for the twins
to run for help. Kaleb and Katarina
ran to Mariposa's house. The twins
stayed with her until the fire truck
came minutes later. Gary killed
the snake, but the couple was
very sick. The paramedics were
unable to save them.

Susy's parents and Mariposa comforted the twins throughout the difficult mourning time. The adults handled all of the legal proceedings, sold their home, and the orphaned twins moved in with their neighbor, Mariposa when Susy's parents returned north.

Mariposa started homeschooling the twins, and also taught them farming skills. She hired a counselor to help the twins cope with their great loss. Because Mariposa lost her husband and child years ago, she understood the twins' suffering.

Aqua, **Sunny**, and Glisten made their new home around the Wolf Bay area. There was a small dragon community living there. Glisten was still small for her age; however, she loved to talk in her dragon language with her friends and to fly for hours.

The dragons loved this area because there was abundant food and woodlands shielded the fields from human view. Other dragons were usually not a threat, but often, humans meant death to dragons. Thankfully, as the dragons flew, they observed very few humans living in the estuary.

One day, young Glisten and her older friend, Coatl, were flying south because the gusty breezes coming off of the Gulf of Mexico helped them to soar high. Glisten and Coatl, were fantastic gliders, even though they were both small for their ages.

The dragons found it challenging to keep aloft while flying out of sight of humans. Every year, the number of people who vacationed and lived on the gulf coast grew. The dragons now needed to stay away from the coastal areas.

Coatl and Glisten made it safely home. However, Glisten wanted to fly farther west and did not understand why she had this desire. She wanted to go out again later in the day but, Sunny told her not to go because the winds were strong and the coastal waves were high.

Over the next year, Aqua and Sunny became very concerned about restless Glisten. The curious dragon kept encouraging her friends to fly with her about halfway to Week's Bay. Even Glisten's new friend Quetzal, who loved to bask in the sun, flew with Glisten. However, Quetzal and Coatl rarely wanted to go too far west.

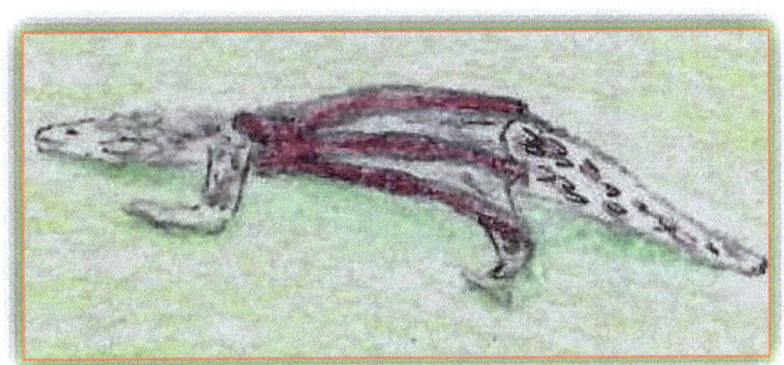

A determined Glisten flew west by herself on a sunny morning when the winds off the gulf were consistently blustery. She took off before her parents awoke. She could no longer fight the urge to fly to the Week's Bay area.

The distance between the dragon community west of Wolf Bay and Week's Bay was about twenty miles. Fortunately, Glisten felt energized since Aqua brought a large fish and Sunny collected several turtle eggs for dinner the night before. Glisten felt she could fly for hours.

When **Sunny** and **Aqua** noticed
Glisten was gone, they alerted the
dragon community. Four dragons
helped look for Glisten; two flew
west and two flew south because
Sunny and **Aqua** knew Glisten
usually flew in those two directions.

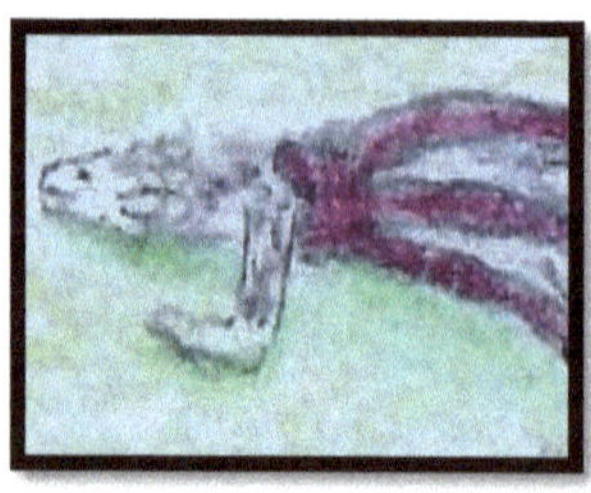

After an entire day of searching, none of the dragons could find her. They rested the next day. The following morning, the dragons continued their search. Little did they know, Glisten flew to the barn on the farm where she was born.

The dragon community did not find her and they were extremely sad. Although Glisten was apart from her parents and friends, she decided to stay on the farm. She had no idea of the new friendships ahead in her future.

Within days, she hid in a smaller barn on the farm property. She was not frightened by the cow who slept there. However, when a young boy entered the barn, she was frightened and burrowed into the straw. The human Glisten saw was Kaleb.

www.ingramcontent.com/pod-product-compliance
Lightning Source LLC
Chambersburg PA
CBHW050441200726
48295CB00024B/936